Danny Can Sort

written and photographed
by
Mia Coulton

Look at the treats.

Look at the treats.

The red treats

are here.

Look at the treats.

The yellow treats

are here.

The green treats

are here.

The orange treats
are here.

Look at
the orange treats.

The treats are not here.